# Daniel Defoe

# ROBINSON CRUSOE

TORMONT

# IN ROBINSON CRUSOE'S DAY...

*A seventeenth century cargo ship*

*Two types of raft, made of different-sized tree trunks*

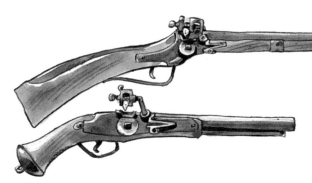

*Shotgun and pistol*

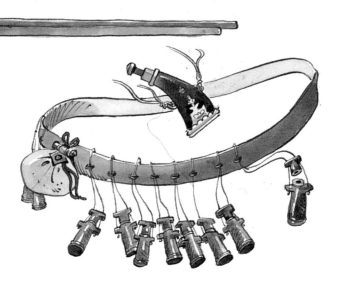

*Ammunition belt, worn over the shoulder, with a gold-trimmed powder horn, a pouch for bullets, and cartridges for loading the gunpowder*

*Animal trap made of saplings*

*Frame for drying animal skins*

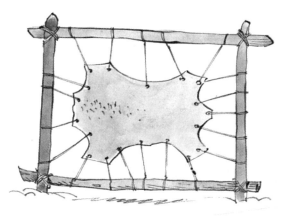

*Native people making a dugout canoe by burning out the middle of a tree trunk, then finishing the work with stone axes*

# THE AUTHOR: DANIEL DEFOE

*Daniel Defoe is known as the father of the modern English novel. He was born in London in 1659. His parents were very strict Protestants. They hoped he would become a minister, and sent him to a very good school. Instead, he became a merchant, but he soon put his excellent education to use in other ways.*

*Long before becoming a novelist, Defoe had gained fame as a political writer. He supported the English reformers, known as the Whigs, and suggested changes that were far ahead of his time, such as higher education for women. He was often in trouble because of his political writing, and had even been sent to prison.*

*It wasn't until 1719, when Defoe was 59, that he published his first novel,* **Robinson Crusoe**. *It told the story of a man shipwrecked off the coast of Brazil. The book was written in the form of a diary, and the name "Robinson Crusoe" appeared on the cover as the author.*

*This was an unusual kind of book for those days. Readers weren't used to novels that seemed so realistic, especially ones with a modern hero who was able to survive far away from civilization.*

*After the success of Robinson Crusoe, Defoe continued to write novels with the same spirit of survival. Among the best known are* **Journal of the Plague Year** *and* **Moll Flanders**. *In 1724, he published a travel book called* **A New Voyage Around the World**. *Defoe himself hadn't traveled widely, but this didn't seem to bother his readers!*

*Until his last years, Defoe lived a fairly comfortable life, despite sometimes being poor. He died near London in 1731. In the two and a half centuries since that time,* **Robinson Crusoe** *has perhaps sold more copies than any book except the Bible. Many versions of this engaging story have been published for children, who continue to enjoy it as a tale of challenge and personal courage.*

# Robinson Crusoe Sets Sail for the First Time

Robinson Crusoe was born in 1632 in the city of York, in England. His one ambition since childhood had been to go to sea.

"Be careful, Rob," his father said, "your elder brother didn't listen to my advice. He became a soldier and was killed in battle. If you don't listen to me now, who knows what will happen to you?"

Still, the longing persisted. When Crusoe was eighteen years old, he found himself drawn to a life of adventure.

One day he was walking in the city of Hull, where he had gone to admire the ships anchored in the port. He didn't plan to go to sea that day; he just wanted to look at the boats and talk to some of the sailors.

But he met a friend in a tavern who persuaded him to board a ship.

And so, without telling anyone, Robinson Crusoe walked up a gangplank and set sail on September 1, 1651.

Crusoe traveled the seas for some time. At last, after many adventures, he settled in Brazil. There, he started a sugar plantation. Some time later, he set sail again, heading for Africa on business.

The ship was a 120-ton cargo boat, with six cannons and a crew of fourteen men, apart from the captain and Robinson Crusoe.

## A STORM AT SEA

Soon, a terrible storm arose. The boat was tossed about like a toy among the huge waves. Rain fell in torrents from the steely sky, while thunder and lightning crashed all around them.

The storm lasted twelve days and swept the ship so far off course that the captain had no idea where they were. Then, one morning, the lookout shouted, "Land ahoy! Land ahoy!"

The sea was still very rough, and the boat was in danger of being dashed to pieces if it struck the rocks along the shore. The captain and crew watched helplessly as their ship came nearer and nearer to the coast.

Suddenly the ship struck a sandbank.

"Every man for himself!" cried the captain. The sailors tried to escape, throwing the lifeboats overboard and jumping into them. Then, with a terrifying roar, an enormous wave washed over men and boats. Robinson Crusoe thrashed his arms and legs about in a desperate attempt to stay afloat. A second wave hurled him forward again. His feet touched bottom. The shipwrecked man staggered through the churning water and collapsed on the shore.

## ROBINSON CRUSOE IS SAVED

Gradually the storm passed. Crusoe opened his eyes.

"Where am I?" was his first thought.

Slowly, he got to his knees, then rose to his feet. He was standing on a wide, sandy beach.

Suddenly he remembered everything – the storm, the shipwreck, giving up hope. . . .

"I'm saved! I'm saved!"

Then he stopped shouting. On the sand lay two odd shoes and a sailor's cap full of water. Crusoe looked all around. There was no one else on the beach or among the nearby trees, or in the sea.

"So I'm the only one saved," thought Crusoe, "and all the others are dead!" He stumbled forward and gazed out to sea. There, on the distant sandbank, the ship lay on its side. The masts were broken and the sails in tatters.

Crusoe burst into tears, feeling all was indeed lost.

After a while, however, he began to regain courage. He felt in his pockets, and there he found a knife, a pipe and a tin box. He opened it, hoping there would be something to eat inside. It was full of tobacco.

"A knife, a pipe, and some tobacco," he muttered, beginning to shiver. "Good God! Have I been saved from the sea only to die of hunger?"

But it was cold, not fear, that made him shiver.

The sun was setting and the evening air was chilly. Crusoe realized he must find somewhere to sleep. First of all, however, he desperately needed water.

Leaving the beach, he threaded his way through the trees and soon recognized a familiar sound – the gurgle of a stream! With a gasp of joy, he kneeled beside the brook and scooped up the cool water.

With his thirst quenched, Crusoe looked around for somewhere to spend the night. Not knowing what wild animals he might have to fear, he climbed a tree and slept as best he could.

It was broad daylight when he awoke. A light breeze was blowing. Hundreds of birds were singing in the trees as Crusoe climbed down from his shelter, stretched, and saw that it was a clear, bright morning. He returned to the beach and, to his great surprise, found that the ship had been lifted off the sandbank by the tide. Now it was floating, not far from shore.

Crusoe tore off his ragged clothes and swam out to the hull. There, on the deck, stood the ship's dog, watching him and whimpering piteously.

"Are you all alone, poor fellow?" asked Crusoe as he climbed aboard the ship and stroked the dog. His only answer was the shriek of gulls circling overhead.

"Hello!" he shouted. "Is there anyone aboard?"

Crusoe went below deck and saw that the cargo had not been damaged in the storm. "Well," he said (for he was beginning to get in the habit of talking to himself), "there are lots of useful things here, but I need a boat to get them back to the shore. Another storm could sweep everything away. I'll build myself a raft."

Crusoe set to work, using his knife. In a few hours, he had tied some of the ship's timbers together with rope and had attached kegs to make floats for his raft. By sunset, he had loaded supplies and pushed off from the ship. Steering with only a makeshift oar, he managed to reach shore before dark.

"I wonder where in the world I am!" he said as he unloaded his precious cargo. "Perhaps this is an uninhabited land. Maybe savages live here."

# ROBINSON CRUSOE SETTLES IN

The sun rose next morning in a cloudless sky. Crusoe was determined to find out were he had ended up. He took a gun from his cargo and set off toward a hill overlooking the beach. Up, up, he climbed until he reached the top. From where he stood, he could look all around. Sea, everywhere. He was on an island! There was no village to be seen, no sign of human life at all.

"And no man-eating beasts, or I'd have seen them by now," he muttered, "but plenty of animals for food!" He raised his gun and shot at a large bird perched in a nearby tree.

At the sound of the gunshot, flocks of birds rose up. Hearing the noise of all those wings, Crusoe felt as though he'd fired the first shot heard on this island since the beginning of the world.

Later in the day, he began to make a list of all the things he'd salvaged from the ship. Food first of all: bread, biscuits, rice, three kinds of Dutch cheese, and some dried goat's meat. Then there were a few bottles of rum, some clothing, knives and forks, about a dozen axes, iron bars, a grindstone for sharpening knives, a hammock, a mattress, a box of carpenter's tools, sacks of nails, chains, sails, shotguns, pistols, barrels of gunpowder . . . but no candles!

"There must be candles somewhere," he said, rummaging through the remaining supplies. "What's in this canvas bag? Ah – chicken feed. Now what can I do with that? And in this box? Books! And here? Money! What use is money now?" he cried, plunging his hands into a chest filled with silver and gold coins. "If I'd known what it was, I'd have left it on the ship!"

Crusoe found a steep cliff on the side of the hill overlooking the sea. There was a hollow in the rock, almost like a cave, and here Crusoe set up a makeshift tent made from a sail. He carried all his supplies up the hill to his new home and stored them safely under the canvas. As he worked he said to himself, "I'm completely alone. There isn't a soul to speak to!"

Next day, Crusoe set up a post on the beach and carved on it the following words: "I came on shore here on the 30th of September, 1659."

Later, when he got back to his camp, he took a notebook, a pen and a pot of ink from one of the boxes, and wrote: "September 30, 1659. I, poor miserable Robinson Crusoe, shipwrecked during a dreadful storm, came on shore on this unfortunate island, which I called the Island of Despair."

Crusoe did not despair, however. He managed to keep his spirits up because he had a goal. He hoped that, by using his energy and skill, he might be able to live like a civilized man and not as a savage.

First, he used his axes to make the cave wider and deeper. Then he set to work making the things he felt were needed most: a table and a chair. As he worked, he made plans to build a fence all around his tent. True, he'd seen no wild beasts, but there might be some lurking in an unknown part of the island.

Soon he had cut a number of young trees for stakes. For the next few days he worked very hard at building a fence. He also made a ladder for climbing in and out of his camp.

Every morning, before setting to work, he took his gun and went off hunting with his dog.

He often came across large nests full of eggs, which made a pleasant change from his normal diet. Soon he found that there were goats wandering in the island's natural meadows. He tried to catch one, but it wasn't easy.

Crusoe wasted no time. After a month, his tent was so well organized that it almost looked like a proper house inside.

He hung his clothes on nails hammered into poles, and arranged many of his possessions on newly-made shelves. The table and chair were finally finished, and Crusoe enjoyed sitting comfortably at sunset, eating his supper or writing his diary.

Through it all, however, he continued to feel a deep sadness, and his gaze constantly scanned the horizon, hoping a ship would appear. Weeks and months passed, but he saw not a single sail. Crusoe marked off the days by cutting notches on the post. As the notches grew in number, his sadness increased. Was he condemned to live like this, separated forever from the rest of the world? He never lost courage, but he looked for strength only within himself because his faith in God was weak. Although he prayed to Him in moments of need, he always forgot about Him soon afterward.

He did not even remember God when, one night, something dreadful and unexpected happened.

A tropical storm had blown up. The rain beat down on his shelter, and the sky was filled with thunder and lightning. Crusoe was lying in bed when suddenly a bolt of lightning struck just outside his tent.

"My gunpowder!" cried Crusoe, terrified. What would have happened if the lightning had struck one of the barrels? There would have been an explosion, and Crusoe would have been killed.

He spent the rest of the night crouched in a corner, trembling. The next morning he worked frantically, putting the gunpowder into boxes, tins, and bags – anything small that could be stored easily and safely inside the cave.

Then, thinking of his general safety, he began strengthening his fence. He worked methodically from morning to night each day. When he was finished, he felt as safe inside his camp as in a fortress.

One day when he was out hunting goats, he shot and killed one. Too late, he realized it was the mother of a kid. He found the little animal nearby, bleating pitifully.

"There, there," he said. "Come with me, and you'll be the first of my new herd." And that was how Robinson Crusoe became a goat farmer!

## Robinson Crusoe Finds New Faith in God

Some weeks later, when he got up one mild morning, Crusoe was astonished to discover a few pale green shoots growing in the earth in front of his tent.

"Goodness!" he cried. "Unless I'm much mistaken, this is barley! Good Lord! Why – it's a miracle!" He lifted his gaze to the sky.

"Thank you, Lord," he said fervently. "You have made barley grow right in front of my house, so that I'll have food."

It was only later that he remembered emptying one of the sacks of chicken feed at just that spot. He'd done it after the lightning storm, so that he could use the sack for gunpowder.

"Of course! A few grains of barley must have fallen and taken root. . . . So it isn't a miracle after all."

All the same, he decided to take very good care of these barley plants. He began to clear a space for planting more seeds. When his axes became blunt, he learned how to turn the grindstone to sharpen them. Later, he invented a mechanism out of rope and string that turned the wheel by itself.

Luckily, the wreck still lay within easy reach from the shore. Crusoe often returned to it to get wood planks, more nails, screws, bits of iron, and other scrap. He had a plan: he wanted to build a boat and escape from the island if possible.

On his way down to the sea one day, he saw a huge turtle crawling across the beach. Although there were plenty of turtles on the island, it was the first turtle he had seen. As he was to discover later, they lived on the other side.

Crusoe grabbed the turtle, turned it over, and killed it.

He spent all day cooking his catch. After eating so much goat's meat, the turtle meat seemed like the tenderest thing he'd ever tasted! Inside the turtle he found sixty eggs, and these, too, were good to eat.

"Perhaps," he thought to himself, "life on this island isn't so dreadful after all."

But then something happened which nearly made him die of fright.

One rainy day, he was hollowing out the cave wall with a pick-axe when suddenly a large piece of earth fell on top of him. He just managed to avoid it and save himself from being buried alive.

Crusoe rushed outside, only to find the earth shaking beneath his feet. An earthquake! It began to rain more heavily. In his terror, he thought of moving his camp, but soon realized that he was probably safer where he was.

His hardships were not over, however. That evening, he began to shiver. It had rained all day, and he had stayed inside his tent making a stool. "It must be the cold," he said to himself. But it wasn't the cold.

A little later, more shivering and a headache told him that he had a fever. "A fever! I'm ill!" said Crusoe. "Who will look after me?"

The fever got worse. Crusoe could not stand up. The shivering continued, and he broke out in a cold sweat. He was very frightened. What would happen to him? Would he die here, all alone?

Oh, how ungrateful he had been to God! He had never thanked Him for all His goodness. Now God's vengeance had struck him. Lying helplessly in his hammock, Crusoe began to pray.

Then he closed his eyes. When he awoke, the fever had gone.

It was a sunny afternoon. Normally, he would have stepped outside for a breath of fresh air. Instead, he took

his copy of the Bible down from a shelf and started to read it.

This time his promise to God was not quickly forgotten. From that moment on, he renewed his faith in the Lord, and placed all his trust in Him.

## Exploring the Island

Many months had passed since the shipwreck. Crusoe now set about exploring his kingdom – or rather, his prison.

Each day he set off with a gun to visit a new part of the island, always accompanied by his faithful dog. Later, in his diary, he noted down hills, ponds, streams, big trees, and other landmarks.

One day, wandering through green meadows and pleasant woods, he came upon a place that resembled a little corner of paradise. All sorts of

plants grew there. Among them, he recognized green tobacco and sugar cane growing wild. On another day, he found melons and cedar trees, and was surprised to see a large vine covered with bunches of dark, shiny fruit.

"These are grapes!" he exclaimed, astonished. He filled his mouth with the sweet, juicy fruit, but limited himself to only one or two bunches, for fear of making himself sick. The rest he hung in the sun to dry, and soon he had a year's supply of raisins.

"In fact," he thought, "I am the king of this island. I own it. I can do whatever I like here. I'm like an English lord! I already have one house. I can have another, a country house!"

So, close to the place where he'd found the grapes, Crusoe built himself a wooden cabin, and here he would go on the hottest days.

Meanwhile he continued to explore the island, and one day he got right to the other side.

Soon he realized that this farther shore was much more hospitable. There were lots of turtles and goats here, as well as a wide variety of birds. Nevertheless, he always considered his hill camp as home, and always returned to it.

Perhaps, deep in his heart, he hoped that his side of the island wasn't too far off the route taken by ships traveling between America and Africa. Sooner or later another survivor from a shipwreck might come ashore. Perhaps, one day, a ship might come into his bay.

# LAND!

The solitude made Crusoe think long and hard about his life. He thanked God for making him realize that he could survive and find some happiness on his lonely island. Whenever he began to feel sad, he would open the Bible and read these words: "I will never, never leave thee, nor forsake thee."

He ate almost nothing but goat's meat. With the animal's fat, he succeeded in making a primitive oil lamp. Of course, it didn't shed the clear, steady light of a wax candle, but now he was no longer a prisoner of the night, obliged to go to sleep after sunset. He could stay awake as long as he wanted, and often spent the evenings making wicker baskets for his supply of raisins.

One day when he was marking another notch on the post, Crusoe realized that a whole year had passed since his arrival. He returned to his house, feeling dejected, but soon the thought of work to be done raised his spirits. He went out to hoe a small plot close by.

Crusoe had made his hoe out of tools from the ship, and now he was preparing the earth for a crop. He had kept the grains of barley which the miraculous plants had produced earlier.

"I'll sow them," Crusoe had said to himself, "and then collect the seeds for new plants. Who knows! Perhaps one day I'll be able to make bread."

The amateur farmer took note of the changing seasons on the island. There was a wet period, when it rained a great deal, followed by a long dry season.

Now, Crusoe sowed the barley seeds in his freshly-hoed plot. Soon after, he was delighted to see shoots poking up through the earth.

On one very clear day, he climbed to the top of the highest hill. From there he could see a faint line, far away on the horizon.

"Land!" cried Crusoe. "America! Perhaps it's Spanish territory. In that case, I'll see ships one day. If it's a savage country, there'll be cannibals. Thank God I've landed on this deserted island!"

# POLL THE PARROT

Suddenly he heard a loud squawking and the sound of beating wings amid rustling leaves.

"Parrots!" exclaimed Crusoe. Using his gun as a stick, he hit the tree as high up as he could. The birds flew off, but one had been knocked on the head and fell out of the tree.

"I didn't mean to kill you, my friend," said Crusoe, picking up the bird. "Oh, not dead? Well, come along then!"

He carefully put the bird into his hunting pouch and started off again. When he returned to his camp, he brought with him the parrot, whom he had christened Poll, and also another little goat which he put in the pen with the first one.

It was wonderful to see how happy all the animals were! In the next few days Crusoe started to make a cage for Poll, who was now fully recovered and tied to a post by one leg. As he worked, weaving the cane, Crusoe would turn to the bird and say:

"Do you know what I'm making, Poll? A cage for you. Just you see how happy you'll be in it." But then he fell silent, thinking, "But this cage will be a prison for you Poll, not a home. Perhaps you'd like to go back to the forest as much as I want to go back to the civilized world. Well, let's see."

He got up and untied the parrot. "There you are, Poll. You're free to leave!"

Poll croaked a little and flew clumsily toward Crusoe.

Delighted, he cried, "You'll stay! I'll make you a perch instead of a cage!"

The weeks and months passed. It was now almost two years since Crusoe had arrived on the island.

"Do you know what this is Poll?" he asked the faithful parrot as the bird watched him working one day. " It's a sword. I'm going to use it as a scythe, and I'll harvest my barley with it!"

Once the barley was harvested, Crusoe had a bright idea for storing it. He would make clay pots.

Crusoe had never modeled clay before. In fact, at first he could hardly tell clay from any other kind of soil.

He patiently searched the island for the right material, then he made some rough pots from it and put them out in the sun to bake. Many broke in the heat of the tropical sun, but others dried perfectly.

His house was now comfortable, spacious, and in good order. It was surrounded by a fence, and outside this he had planted a line of small trees.

The tent opened into the cave, where Crusoe had hollowed out several rooms.

Wooden partitions divided the living space from the storage area. He had a bedroom and a workshop. One little room was filled with guns and pistols.

In another room he kept the wicker baskets, full of raisins or dried meat, and also clay pots filled with barley.

Crusoe wasn't content with making the rather breakable pots of sun-dried clay. After a great deal of hard work, he managed to build an oven for baking the clay properly. Soon he was making tiles and building himself a real fireplace.

He also managed to make clay cooking pots. After eating grilled meat for two years, he finally tasted delicious turtle stew!

Crusoe had an even more ambitious plan: to make bread. For this, he needed an unbreakable bowl for grinding the grain. He made it by hollowing out a large block of very hard wood. To sift the flour from the barley husks, he nailed a piece of muslin onto a wicker frame.

When at last he had made the flour, Crusoe added water to it and worked it into a dough. He patted the dough into loaves, put them on the hot tiles of the fireplace, and covered them with some large, oblong pots. These were in turn covered with redhot embers. Later, he swept away the embers and lifted off the pots.

Bread! As tasty as any from a fine baker's shop!

# A Canoe Trip Around the Island

Crusoe's supply of clothes was becoming threadbare. For some time, his last shirt had been too ragged to wear. His jacket and trousers were also in a pitiful state.

He had stretched animal skins on frames to dry, and now decided to use these to make himself a new outfit. He was no tailor, but managed to piece together a hat to protect his head from rain and sun, a loose tunic, a pair of wide trousers, and even an umbrella. "I must make an odd sight," he thought, once his new clothes were finished.

Five years had passed since the shipwreck. Crusoe watched the horizon every day, hoping to see a sail appear. Finally he decided to make himself a canoe. Perhaps one day he would embark on the great journey to the civilized world!

For the moment, he was happy to make a less demanding journey. Hollowing out a tree trunk with the aid of fire and axe, he produced a dugout canoe such as he had seen the Indians of Brazil make.

In this new vessel, complete with a little sail, Crusoe set off for a trip around the island. At first it was an easy journey. How beautiful the island seemed, with its cliffs and white beaches! There were hills and rocks that he'd never seen before. He cast anchor and rested in shady little bays. His adventure seemed delightful – until, on the fourth day, he found himself in great danger.

The canoe was suddenly caught up in a strong current, and soon the island was left far behind.

The wind dropped. Without warning, large black clouds appeared on the horizon.

"Oh, miserable creature that I am!" groaned Crusoe, with tears in his eyes. "Why have I come here? I was so happy in my house. What will happen to this little boat if a storm blows up? And where will this current carry me?"

He had almost lost hope when a stiff breeze sprang up. Skillfully using his little sail, Crusoe succeeded in moving against the dangerous current, and at last steered a course toward the island.

He landed in a little cove and lay down, exhausted, under a tree. When he had rested, he climbed into his canoe again. Keeping as close as possible to the shore, he made his way home.

As he clambered over his fence and found himself in familiar surroundings, he felt a surge of joy. He was about to throw himself on his bed when a voice cried:

"Robin, Robin! Robin Crusoe!"

"Good God! Who's that?" exclaimed Crusoe. He glanced around, alarmed and curious.

"Robin Crusoe!" the voice repeated. "Poor Robin Crusoe, where are you? Where have you been?" and Poll the parrot flew toward him and landed at his feet.

"What a fright you gave me, Poll!" said Crusoe, picking up the bird and stroking her. "But it's nice to hear another voice for a change!"

# A Human Footprint

Many years went by, and Crusoe became accustomed to his island life. He realized how difficult it might be to return to the world he'd known before the shipwreck.

His former life seemed very far away, and there appeared to be little hope of ever seeing the shores of England again. No – he must resign himself to staying on the island.

But during the eleventh year, he made a discovery that astonished and frightened him.

One morning, he set off hunting as usual. He walked along between the forest and the beach, singing softly to himself, then left the shelter of the trees and walked toward the water's edge.

Suddenly he stopped and stared in disbelief at the ground.

It couldn't be!

Clearly outlined on the sand was a human footprint!

Crusoe shook his head, then looked again. He raised his gun and turned around. There was no one to be seen anywhere.

He slowly crossed the beach, searching for more footprints, always keeping a wary eye on the sea and the forest.

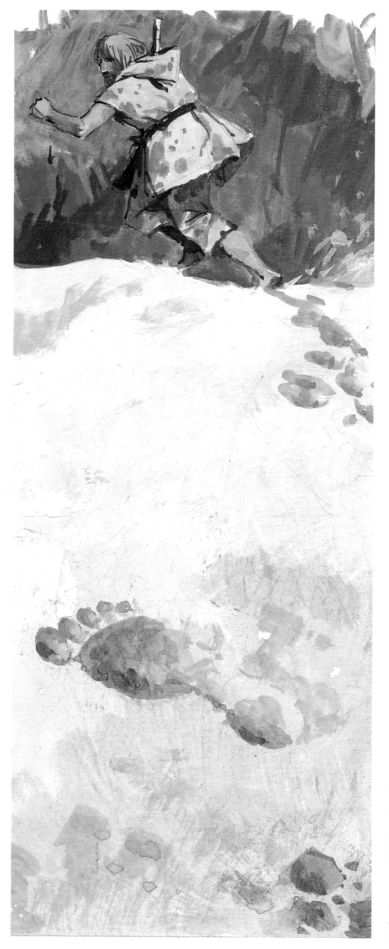

"But how is it possible?" he asked himself. "Who can have arrived on this island? Someone certainly has! So, there is someone else here as well as myself. Or perhaps," he thought suddenly, "my mind is playing tricks on me."

He retraced his steps. The footprint was still there.

He stared at it, then compared it with his own. It certainly wasn't *his* footprint.

Overcome with fear, Crusoe fled like a frightened hare, stumbling and falling repeatedly in his panic.

He ran through the wood that had grown around the fence over the years, clambered up the ladder, and fell into the goat pen. He scrambled to his feet and peered over the fence.

Nothing. He held his breath, listening.

The birds were singing as usual. Every tree, every bush was motionless.

Crusoe did not move. The sun rose high in the sky, then started to sink. It was growing dark, and Crusoe was still on guard.

"Perhaps it was the devil? No, the devil doesn't leave footprints! And anyway, if he had wanted to frighten me, he wouldn't have been foolish enough to leave a footprint on the sand, where it would be washed away by the sea. Bare feet . . . a savage! Perhaps cannibals have come to the island, have seen my boat . . . or discovered my shelter!"

He kept his eyes open as long as he could, but finally fell asleep, holding his gun.

When Crusoe awoke, he was still very frightened. Any cannibals who landed on the island would easily follow his tracks, and would see his barley field and the goat pen. For an instant, he thought of knocking down the goat pen, setting the animals free, and destroying his barley field.

Soon, however, common sense won out. He plucked up his courage. With a pistol stuck in his belt and a shotgun on his arm, he ventured out to look around the island.

He saw nothing unusual. There seemed to be no one around but turtles and birds. On the beach, he stopped to look at the footprint, and finally returned home, feeling deeply worried.

Then, as if guided by God, he took down the Bible from its shelf. He opened it and read these words: "Wait on the Lord, and be of good cheer, and He shall strengthen thy heart."

This gave him great comfort. He began to think calmly. Possibly the island was inhabited, even though he'd found no trace of it. If so, he might easily have been attacked at any time.

Now that he had seen land on the distant horizon, he knew that people might sometimes land on his island. He would have to make plans for greater safety.

## CRUSOE STRENGTHENS HIS DEFENSES

The next day he set to work to strengthen the defenses around his camp. He added new posts to the fence, and made about five or six slits in it for shotguns.

Then he began to plant iron stakes all around the fence, to create a good strong barricade, and he camouflaged the goat pen with branches and leaves.

"I must hide my canoe, too," thought Crusoe. He left his house, carrying a shotgun that was primed and ready to fire, and crept down to the shore where his canoe was tied. He pulled it through the shallow waves and into the reeds of a small cove. After that, he crept home, keeping a sharp lookout the whole time.

When he reached the stockade, he heard the goats bleating. "I must milk them," he thought. He did this, and afterward went to the spring for a fresh water supply. In no time, he was going about his usual routine and leading a normal life again.

Many months passed, and nothing happened.

# THE CAVE

Even though no danger arose during this time, Crusoe no longer dared light a wood fire close to his home, for fear someone might spot it.

Then, realizing he must cook in order to eat, he taught himself how to make a smokeless kind of fuel. As he had seen people do in England, he made wood fires far away from home, and reduced the wood to charcoal by burning it under a layer of turf. Once this was done, he put out the fires and took the charcoal home.

Crusoe also chanced upon a safe shelter for his most precious belongings – his weapons, gunpowder, tools, and seeds.

This is how he found it. One day, when he was out looking for wood, he discovered the opening to a cave at the bottom of a cliff.

It was hidden by thick bushes, but he managed to get through and found himself in a small cave. At the back, he could see two eyes shining like stars.

He jumped back outside, terrified. Then he pulled himself together. After all these years on the island, surely there was nothing more that could frighten him. He lit a firebrand and went back into the cave.

He saw a large old billy goat lying there gasping for breath. It looked as though it had reached the end of its days. Behind the poor animal, Crusoe could make out the mouth of a low tunnel.

He crawled into the tunnel, which soon opened out into a spacious cave with walls that twinkled like gold in the light of the torch. The area against the farther wall was as dry as a bone: an ideal place to keep all of Crusoe's most precious possessions safe.


# A CANNIBAL FEAST


Crusoe no longer dared to fire his gun, afraid that someone might hear. This meant he had to learn to hunt using traps.

One day, he went out to see if a goat had fallen into a certain trap that he had carefully dug and covered with leaves. When he reached the top of a hill he looked out, as usual, toward the sea.

All at once he stopped. Something was out there, on the horizon.

"Good God!" he exclaimed, his voice shaking, "there's a canoe heading away from the island!"

He loaded his gun and, on the alert, came down from the hill to patrol the beach. A fire was burning on the sand some distance away. Trembling with fear, he walked slowly toward it.

What he saw filled him with horror: bloodstains and human skeletons, the remains of a grisly feast!

Crusoe was in no doubt. Cannibals had landed on the island and had eaten their fellow human beings. He was terrified.

"Cannibals! I've been on this island for eighteen years now, and I've never seen these wretches. Heaven knows how many times they've been here!"

Soon, however, he managed to look at things more calmly.

"Perhaps they only come here to kill and eat their prisoners," he muttered. "I may not see another human footprint for the next eighteen years."

Reassured, he went on with his walk.

Nevertheless, he still went about armed with a loaded gun, and he made a point of looking out to sea before going down to the shore. Then, one December day in the twenty-third year of his stay on the island, something happened that changed his life.

Crusoe was heading off to work in his barley field, his scythe on his shoulder, when a strange light caught his attention. He stopped and looked anxiously toward the beach. There was a large fire burning there!

This time the savages had landed close to where he lived!

He raced home and began preparing for his defense. First he pulled the ladder inside his stockade, placed guns in all the slits, and then sat down to wait.

For at least two hours he remained there, expecting something to happen. Finally, he couldn't bear the suspense any longer. He had to find out what was going on.

Taking a telescope – one of his treasures saved from the wreck – he cautiously climbed the hill and surveyed the scene below.

There was indeed a fire. Around it, he could make out the dark figures of at least nine savages. They certainly hadn't lighted a fire to warm themselves, for the weather was hot. It was to cook some dreadful meal made of human flesh!

The savages had two canoes with them, and these had been pulled up onto the beach. It being low tide, Crusoe thought they must be waiting until the tide came in before leaving.

This proved to be the case. The black figures danced for over an hour, but as soon as the tide started to come in, they pushed their canoes out into the surf and paddled furiously to get beyond the sand bank.

Thanks to his telescope, Crusoe had been able to see their gestures and facial expressions, but he had no idea what they might mean.

As soon as he saw the cannibals disappear, he picked up his weapons and ran down to the beach as fast as he could. He was horrified by the gruesome remains of the feast strewn around the fire. Hands, feet, and skulls lay about in heaps.

So angered was he by the sight, that he began to imagine ways of attacking and killing the cannibals when they next visited the island. However, he soon realized what an impossible task it would be.

From that day on, he slept badly, dreaming of horrors and waking with a start. Yet strange to say, the sight of these other humans, however sickening, had begun to make him long for human companionship.

# THE SHIP
# ON THE ROCKS

A year went by uneventfully. Then, one night, a dreadful storm blew up. Thunder shook the sky, and lightning flashed, lighting up the sky like fireworks.

In his shelter, Crusoe was reading by the flickering light of his goat's-fat lamps, when suddenly the air was shaken by a gunshot.

A gunshot! He jumped to his feet and ran out. The wind carried the sound of another gunshot.

"They're shooting from the sea!" he exclaimed. "It must be a ship in distress! I must do something – I'll signal to them that there is an island here. If they're saved, I will be, too!"

So he climbed the hill and started to collect branches and dry grass for a fire. The wind fed the blaze, and soon he had a beacon of crackling yellow flames.

Although he knew nobody could hear him, Crusoe shouted, "Mind the rocks! Make sure you don't end up on the rocks!"

He heard more gunshots. The sailors on the storm-tossed ship must have seen his beacon, and they were shooting to ask for more help.

But what help could one lone man give them? The only thing that Crusoe could do was to keep the fire alight until daybreak.

When the morning finally came and the sky grew light, Crusoe saw a boat on the sea, a long way away. But he could not tell what kind of ship it was because of the haze over the water.

As the hours passed he realized that the boat hadn't moved from its position, and he thought it must be anchored. Taking his gun, he set off in his canoe. Poll the parrot went with him, perched on his shoulder.

## DISAPPOINTMENT

As Crusoe drew near, he saw that the ship had been cast upon the rocks and was now stuck fast amid the waves.

"Anyone aboard?" he shouted. But there was no reply. Dismayed, he began to think that perhaps everyone was dead. The bridge of the boat was completely deserted.

When he climbed onto the ship, he again shouted, "Anyone aboard?" Except for the wind and the waves, nothing stirred.

It looked like a Spanish ship. Crusoe explored as much as he could, gathering precious supplies to take home. As he went through the ship, he came upon the bodies of two sailors. It seemed that those who weren't trapped in the boat must have been swept away in the storm.

That night he slept in his boat. Next morning, he decided to hide the articles taken from the wreck in his new cave. Afterward, he paddled his canoe back to its hidden bay.

# A FRIEND

Now, more than ever, Crusoe longed for companionship. Somehow, he must find a friend – not only as someone to talk to, but as a helper to build a proper boat, big enough to get back to civilized shores.

Of course, the best thing would be to find a man who knew the mainland coast. . . .

"A savage!" Crusoe said to himself. "I must capture a savage!"

Every day, he climbed the hill to look out over the sea. Despite his fears, he almost looked forward to seeing a cannibal canoe!

For many months he saw no sign of a vessel. At last came the day when he saw five canoes approaching. Crusoe ran into his house to fetch his telescope and two loaded guns, and hid in the bushes to watch.

Two men were being dragged ashore by copper-colored savages. The poor souls were clearly about to be killed and devoured by these Indians – but wait! He saw one of the dark-skinned victims wrench himself free, then take off as though the devil were at his heels, chased by two of the cannibals. He was heading straight for the wood where Crusoe was hiding!

Crusoe grabbed a gun and stepped out between the fugitive and his pursuers. He stunned the first cannibal, then shot the second.

The runaway stopped, terrified and astonished at the sudden appearance of this strange white man who killed people with a magic stick.

There was moment's silence. Then Crusoe gave the runaway an encouraging wave. "Don't be afraid," he said. "Come with me."

The fugitive was too frightened to move. He was clearly terrified that Crusoe would kill him, too.

Crusoe smiled and repeated, with a friendly gesture, "Don't be afraid. I'm your friend! It's too dangerous for us to stay here, you know, so come along with me!"

The black man came forward very slowly, one step at a time.

Then he fell on his knees and placed his head on the ground. As a sign of gratitude and submission, he grabbed Crusoe's foot and placed it on his head.

# FRIDAY

The fugitive said something. Crusoe couldn't understand his speech, but found it delightful all the same. These were the first words spoken to him by another human being in nearly twenty-five years.

"I'm no longer alone!" Crusoe exclaimed thankfully.

"Get up, man!" he urged the fugitive. "We'd better be off before the others find us." Without wasting a moment, Crusoe crept through the underbrush to his camp, followed by his new friend.

"Well, my friend, since we'll be living together, I must give you a name." The man's only response was to kneel down and lay his head beneath Crusoe's foot again.

"Come now, get up! I shall call you Friday – because, according to my calendar, today is Friday." Crusoe pointed his finger at the dark man's chest, "You are Friday. I am Master."

Crusoe repeated these words, pointing now at the savage, now at himself. At last the man said slowly, "Friday . . . Master."

Friday quickly learned to speak and understand Crusoe's language. He was a willing servant, and had great skill with weapons.

"Friday, where do you come from?" Crusoe asked one day.

Friday gestured toward the west. "Come from far land."

Then Crusoe took Friday to see the wreck of the Spanish ship, which was still lying on the rocks, being battered by the sea.

"Do you see that? I came ashore from a boat like that."

Friday looked thoughtful and said, "Friday see boat come to Friday's country." Then he added, "Boat full of white mans. We save them."

Men! White men! Crusoe asked him how many there were.

Friday, counting on his fingers, showed him that there had been seventeen.

Crusoe learned that these people were living in Friday's country, and that the natives had treated the survivors like brothers. From that moment on, he longed to make a sea voyage and find other survivors like himself.

One day he asked Friday, "Would you like to go back to your country, to your people?"

"Oh, yes, but Master come with Friday."

"I wouldn't dream of it!"

"Me not swim that far!" replied Friday, with a smile.

Crusoe insisted. "Take the boat and go if you want; you are free!"

Friday had tears in his eyes and his voice was trembling. "Why you angry mad with Friday? What me done? Why you want to send me away? Look," he said, holding out a hatchet to Crusoe, "take him and kill Friday."

"What? Why should I want to kill you?" cried Crusoe.

Weeping, the savage answered, "What you want to send Friday away for? Kill Friday, no send Friday away!" And he fell on his knees and again put his head beneath his master's foot.

Crusoe was very moved by such a show of faith, and put his hand on the savage's head.

"I can see that you are truly loyal to me."

# The Big Canoe

Now that Crusoe had put his companion's loyalty to the test, he had no fear of asking him to help build a boat on which they could both escape from the island.

The two men began to search for suitable trees for making a large boat that would be able to weather a rough sea.

There was plenty of suitable wood on the island. What they needed were trees growing near the shore.

Friday chose the wood, and Crusoe explained the kind of boat he wanted. The two men worked side by side for several months, building a sturdy boat big enough for twenty men. When it was finished, they pushed it on rollers into the sea.

Crusoe was amazed to see how skillfully Friday maneuvered the boat, turning it easily with a paddle, despite its size.

"But do you really think we can risk a journey in this boat?" he asked Friday, still uncertain about the project.

"Yes, Friday cross sea very well, even if big wind blow."

But Crusoe was not satisfied and wanted to give the boat a mast, a sail, and a rudder. He chose a cedar for the mast, and patched together a triangular sail from old canvas. The rudder was the most difficult of all, but finally it was ready.

Although Friday was an expert paddler, he knew nothing of sailing. He was amazed as he watched Crusoe manipulating sail and rudder to steer with the wind.

By now the rainy season had arrived, and there was no question of setting out on a sea voyage for the moment. They pulled the boat into a creek, safe from storms, and covered it with boughs.

As the rain pelted down outside, the two men spent their days working in the house.

## THE CANNIBALS RETURN

One day, at the start of the warm season, Friday came running into the house, out of breath.

"Master! Master!" he cried, "Oh, sorrow! Oh, bad!"

"What on earth has got into you, Friday?"

"One, two, three canoe come! They come! They come and eat poor Friday!"

"No!" said Crusoe, going to the corner where he kept his guns, "the cannibals will not eat you or me. Here, take a gun and we'll see what's going on. Friday . . . we may have to fight. Can you fight?"

Friday took the gun which Crusoe was holding out to him and said, "Me shoot. Me die when you command, Master."

Crusoe loaded several guns and pistols, and the two crept into the woods. Hidden among the bushes, Crusoe surveyed the beach through his telescope.

"There are twenty-one cannibals . . . and they've brought two poor fellows with them to eat," he whispered to his companion, who lay beside him on the ground. "Friday, go and check, but don't let them see you."

Friday nodded and disappeared into the tall grass. About twenty minutes later, he came back.

"Them savages eating one man. Them have another man to kill. He white, with beard like you, Master."

At these words, Crusoe started. "Friday, if he's a white man we can't let him die. Quick – we have no time to lose. Do exactly what I tell you."

As they ran toward the beach, they saw a white man lying bound hand and foot. Two cannibals stood by him, knives raised.

"Fire!" shouted Crusoe. He fired at one of the savages. Friday immediately copied him, and the two cannibals fell to the ground. The remaining savages rushed toward their canoes.

Crusoe ran to the prisoner and cut him free.

"Who are you?" he asked the stranger.

"A Christian," replied the other in Spanish.

Crusoe helped the prisoner to his feet and handed him a pistol. "Get ready to fight! The cannibals are coming back."

The savages had indeed overcome their fear and were running toward them, yelling and screaming. A brief, fierce combat followed. Crusoe, Friday, and the prisoner killed all but three of the attackers. The survivors jumped into a canoe and escaped, paddling desperately.

There were two canoes left on the beach. Surprisingly, another victim was lying in one. Friday bent over to untie the man, then suddenly began to leap and shout. "Father!" he cried in his language, hugging and kissing the man in the canoe.

Both the Spaniard and Friday's father were faint with thirst. Friday ran like the wind to fetch a little fresh water and some bread from the house.

The two former victims were half-carried to Crusoe's camp. As they were too weak to climb the ladder over the fence, a temporary tent was set up for them just outside, with beds of fresh straw.

Crusoe made sure they were comfortable, then he sat down to think. He was overjoyed at this turn of events. Now his island was truly inhabited. He felt almost like a king, surrounded by his subjects.

He turned to the Spaniard and asked him how he had come to be imprisoned by the cannibals.

The sailor explained that he was one of the seventeen Spaniards who had landed in Friday's country in a storm. He told Crusoe of the dreadful state in which he and his companions had been found. They'd had nothing – not even a weapon for hunting food.

Friday's people had treated the survivors with hospitable kindness. Later, the Spaniard had wandered outside the tribal lands. He had been captured by a band of hostile Indians.

Crusoe had a proposal to make.

"Would your friends agree to come here and then set off in search of freedom?" he asked the Spaniard. "There would be twenty of us here, including you and your friends, Friday and his father, and myself. We could build a good ship, strong enough to carry us anywhere in the world. What do you say? There'd be just one condition: your friends would have to swear on the Bible to obey my orders."

"They'd gladly agree!" the Spaniard assured Crusoe.

"Then go with Friday's father, and bring them back to the island."

A few days later, the two men set sail for the mainland in Crusoe's boat, carrying food and guns.

"Have a safe journey!" Crusoe cried.

"We'll be back soon!" shouted the Spaniard.

Eight days later, Friday came running to Crusoe's tent. "Master, Master! They are come, they are come!"

## THE MUTINEERS

Crusoe rushed outside without even taking a gun and ran through the woods to the beach. Friday followed right behind.

But all of a sudden Crusoe stopped and crouched down in the undergrowth, telling Friday to do the same.

There, in the bay in front of them, a ship was slowly approaching – but it was not the vessel Crusoe had been expecting. It was clearly a longboat, the kind used by English ships for going ashore.

There were eleven men on board. Crusoe was surprised to see that three of them had their hands tied behind their backs. The newcomers came ashore, roughly pushing their prisoners ahead at sword point.

"Master . . . now white mans eat prisoners," Friday whispered.

"No, Friday, I don't think so, but there's great danger that they'll be killed. Run and get the guns while I wait here."

Friday obeyed. Crusoe crept closer to the men.

They were indeed English. One of them, who seemed to be the leader, said, "We'll finish them off later. Let's go and find some fresh water. These three aren't going anywhere!"

"You're right about that, Will," replied one of the other men.

The three prisoners were pushed into the shade of a large tree, and the rest of the men went off into the forest in search of water.

Crusoe was uncertain what to do next. Friday returned, his arms full of guns.

"Look, Friday," Crusoe said, "the tide is going out and the lifeboat will soon be left high and dry. Will and his friends won't be able to leave. I don't know who the three prisoners are, but I do know there must be a British ship nearby!"

Crusoe's heart was pounding. "I've waited for this day for twenty-eight years. Let's see who these three prisoners are! Follow me, Friday!"

The castaway boldly marched out onto the beach and walked toward the tree where the prisoners lay. As he came up behind them, he said, "Who are you, gentlemen?"

The three men turned round, terrified.

"Don't be surprised at my appearance," said Crusoe with a smile and a friendly gesture, "and don't be afraid. Perhaps you have an unexpected friend in me."

"If you're a friend," whispered one of the prisoners, "you've been sent by heaven."

"Who are you? Why are you tied up?" asked Crusoe.

"I am the captain of an English merchant vessel," the prisoner replied. "My ship is anchored just beyond the end of this island. These gentlemen are my first mate and a passenger. My sailors have mutinied and brought us here to murder us!"

"They won't kill you," Crusoe interrupted. "I'll free you. But you must first swear to obey my orders!"

"We swear it," said the three men solemnly, and Crusoe set them free.

At that moment, Friday cried, "Master, Master, mans arrive!"

And indeed, they could hear voices approaching.

Crusoe gave each man a gun. "Quick, everyone into the bushes!"

Meanwhile the mutineers had appeared at one end of the beach.

"Do you see the tall man?" said the captain. "That's Will, the leader of the mutiny."

"And who are the others? Are they loyal to him?"

"No, they're good men, forced to take part in the mutiny. I'm sure that, given the chance, they would be loyal to me again."

"Get ready, gentlemen!" Crusoe ordered. "We must deal with Will first. At my signal, follow me! And don't waste bullets!"

A few minutes passed, during which the mutineers stopped to look at their boat, now stranded by the tide.

Suddenly Crusoe cried, "Forward!" Jumping out of the bushes, followed by Friday and the three men, he hurled himself at the group of mutineers, firing as he ran.

The mutineers, taken by surprise, put up a brief battle. Will was shot and wounded.

Seeing this, the other mutineers threw down their weapons and put their hands up. "Don't shoot. Mercy! Mercy!" cried one. "We surrender!"

"Captain," said another, "we are your faithful sailors. The others forced us to mutiny."

"I believe you," replied the captain. "Come here."

Three of the sailors came forward immediately, declaring their loyalty. The other four stayed where they were, their hands still in the air.

"Have pity on us, sir!" one of them said.

"I will, but only if you change your ways! Tie them up!" the captain ordered. Turning to Crusoe, he asked, "What are your commands, sir?"

"My advice," replied Crusoe, "is to recapture the ship without delay. How many men are still aboard?"

"Twenty-two, and I can trust some of them."

"Good. If you act quickly and slip onto the ship in the dark with these loyal men, you can surprise the sleeping mutineers."

"Splendid idea! We'll try it. Did you hear that?" he asked his men.

"We're ready!" they chorused.

The captain thanked Crusoe for saving his life. "God grant that we may meet again, my friend," he said. "If you see our ship with the Union Jack flying from the mast, you'll know we've won!"

A short while later Crusoe watched the longboat as it headed slowly out to sea in the fading light.

The men on board would have to approach the ship in the dark. It was a risky plan.

# LEAVING THE ISLAND

It was a long night for Crusoe. He and Friday returned home with the wounded man and the remaining mutineers. Friday stayed awake to guard them.

Crusoe tried to sleep, but in vain. "Oh, faithful Poll!" he said to his parrot. "These hours will decide my fate. If the captain fails, my life will be miserable. I'll have to stay here, but the island will never be the same for me!"

At last he slept, and woke with the dawn. As a rosy light spread through the sky, he ran up the hill with Friday at his side.

Crusoe looked anxiously out to sea. He could see nothing. Then, all at once, a ship sailed around a distant cape and moved slowly toward them. From the mast fluttered the Union Jack!

Crusoe let out a cry of joy. The ship sailed into the bay and cast anchor. The longboat was lowered, and he saw the captain climb into it, along with a group of sailors.

"Them victory!" cried Friday. "Oh joy! Oh journey!"

Meanwhile the captain had come ashore and was shaking Crusoe by the hand. "My friend," he exclaimed, "the ship is safe, thanks to you!"

Crusoe was so overcome at this moment, when he himself was about to be saved, that he broke down and sobbed in the captain's arms. The captain told him how easily they had surprised the mutineers.

Will, the wounded leader, would be taken back to England to be tried for mutiny. The remaining prisoners were given the choice of remaining on the island. The men chose to stay where they were, and to make the best of Crusoe's skillful methods of survival.

"What is today's date?" said Crusoe, turning to the captain.

"December 19th, 1686."

"December 19th, 1686!" exclaimed Crusoe, "That means I've spent twenty-eight years, two months and . . . nineteen days here."

Much moved, he went into his house. There, he found himself surrounded by the things that had been his world for twenty-eight years: the chairs, the table, the tools, the baskets, his storeroom with its pots full of barley – all the things that he had found or made, and that had meant the difference between a becoming a savage or living like a civilized man.

"Master! Master! Oh journey!" said a voice. Crusoe turned to see Friday, dressed in a sailor's uniform.

"Master likes Friday dressed as gentleman?"

"You look very handsome, Friday. It suits you."

Crusoe stayed a while longer in his house then went to the goat pen to say goodbye to the goats.

"The Spaniards will arrive soon, and they'll take care of you," he said. "Who knows, maybe I'll come back one day to see how you're getting on."

He went into his house once more, this time to get his goatskin hat and umbrella as souvenirs of his life on the island. Friday carried out the chest of coins.

From her perch, Poll cried, "Where are you going Robin Crusoe? Poor Robin! Where are you going?"

Picking up the parrot, Crusoe replied, "This time Poll, you're coming too!"

# Home!

The wind was favorable, and the ship continued its trading voyage. It reached London on June 11th, 1687, nearly thirty-six years after Crusoe had first set sail. After all this time, he was now a stranger in his own country.

Crusoe went to York, and there found two sisters still living. His family had long given him up for dead, however. Apart from the coins he had brought back from the island, Crusoe had nothing to live on.

"Oh, Friday, we aren't on our island any more!" he lamented. "To live here we must have money!"

Once again, luck was on his side. The captain had told the ship's owners how Crusoe saved the cargo from the mutineers, and he had persuaded them to give a reward of two hundred pounds. Crusoe used this money to get Friday and himself to Lisbon. There he found an old business partner, who was overjoyed to see him. Yes, the plantation in Brazil was doing well, and half of the profits over the years belonged to Crusoe!

For some years, Crusoe remained at home in England. He took care of two orphaned nephews, got married, and had three children of his own.

At last, in 1694, Crusoe set sail again on a trading mission. On this voyage he visited his island. There he found the Spaniards, who had done well, despite trouble with the mutineers. There were now women in the little colony, and twenty children!

As he sailed away, Crusoe once again thanked God for all His generosity. Despite his strange adventures, with God's help he had proved what one man can achieve by courage and faith.


# The End

© 1991 Dami Editore, Italy
Illustrated by Libico Maraja
Text by Jane Brierley, based on
an adaptation by S. Pazienza

Published in 1994 by
Tormont Publications Inc.
338 Saint Antoine St. East
Montreal, Canada  H2Y 1A3

ISBN 2-89429-586-3

Printed in EEC, Officine Grafiche De Agostini - Novara 1994
Bound by Legatoria del Verbano S.p.A.